Nene's Tales

Ancel Mondia

Ukiyoto Publishing

All global publishing rights are held by

Ukiyoto Publishing

Published in 2023

Content Copyright © Ancel Mondia

ISBN 9789360167783

*All rights reserved.
No part of this publication may be reproduced, transmitted, or stored in a retrieval system, in any form by any means, electronic, mechanical, photocopying, recording or otherwise, without the prior permission of the publisher.*

The moral rights of the authors have been asserted.

This is a work of fiction. Names, characters, businesses, places, events, locales, and incidents are either the products of the author's imagination or used in a fictitious manner. Any resemblance to actual persons, living or dead, or actual events is purely coincidental.

This book is sold subject to the condition that it shall not by way of trade or otherwise, be lent, resold, hired out or otherwise circulated, without the publisher's prior consent, in any form of binding or cover other than that in which it is published.

www.ukiyoto.com

Contents

Salve the Shrimp	1
Minda the Moth	4
Anita the Ant	7
Winona the Worm	10
Selene the Snail	15
Bathilda the Bat	19
About the Author	24

Salve the Shrimp

His steely hands swiftly held her damp fingers. His lips glowed with a smile, and her eyes widened with a spark. Their short bodies were yet to take the shape of teens, but their childlike spirits met like intertwined roots.

The seashore seemed to be their playground as a young man and a young lady, but profoundly was the paradise of their mutual young love. Their little feet scattered the sand, as they delightfully chased each other.

Their thin arms carried stones that they singly threw to the sea. They humorously argued on the distance a ripple could take. After they simultaneously laughed, they exchanged deep stares.

"Salve, do you know how far a ripple goes?" Dante solemnly queried.

"I don't know, Dante." Salve cheerfully replied.

Dante heavily sighed. "That's how far we will go. Together."

Salve turned silent with a puzzled look, as Dante shifted his eyes toward the view of the sunset before them. Tears wetted his sight, but he quickly rubbed his eyes and dried his cheeks. Her face dimmed as her eyes steadily focused on him.

Her lips shivered as she uttered a question. "Are you leaving me?"

He weakly bowed his head. She quietly observed him, and he nodded with hesitation.

They abruptly sobbed with weighty shattered hearts. Throbbing pain contracted their delicate faces. After a while, Dante gradually lifted his head.

"It hurts me to see you cry." He truthfully spoke.

His warm palms wiped away the thick tears on her soft cheeks.

"I'll go, but I'll come back. When I am grown and successful, I'll come back."

Salve nodded with hope, and she embraced Dante tight. They slowly let go of each other, agreeably turned their back, and confusingly walked away.

The darkness of night eventually appeared and seemingly lingered longer.

The expected sunrise heated the abandoned rendezvous, and a middle-aged man in suit emerged. He walked leisurely with a pensive look, and he silently stopped when his longing eyes laid on the back of a woman's hourglass figure. The man's visage lit with certainty, and he broke the silence by clearly pronouncing the name, "Salve."

The woman jerked in surprise, and she swiftly faced the man. Her questioning eyes roved on him, and they exchanged familiar stares. Salve abruptly trembled in fear when she assuredly recognized the man. With pain and love in her voice, she called him, "Dante."

His lips smiled and her eyes sparked as a sign of rekindled romance. Dante walked closer, but Salve stepped back. She seemed to regain consciousness of herself, as she panicked to cover her face.

"What's wrong, Salve?" He asked in confusion.

"Don't look at me!" She screamed in shame.

Dante stood still with a puzzled expression. He gradually noticed that Salve had excess hair on her chest and thick beard on her chin. Dante was apparently shocked by Salve's physical form.

Salve acted crazily, and she dashed into the sea. Dante came to his senses, and attempted to stop her, but the wild waves obstructed him.

Dante emerged from the sea, and Salve was out of sight. All of a sudden, strange creatures floated in the waters. Dante forcefully called Salve's name, and he abruptly recalled her laughter that sounded like the word, shrimp.

Minda the Moth

The party lights flickered and the dance music amplified in an open gymnasium situated at the heart of a rural woodland.

The warm spotlight suddenly focused on a voluptuous woman who discoed at the center of the crowded floor. Her magnetic hips and legs swayed, and her hypnotic chest and arms shook.

She energetically turned around, and a man surprisingly appeared before her. He widely grinned, and his handsome face instantly spellbound her, as if the lights steadied and the music faded.

"What's your name?" The man clearly asked.

The woman softly replied. "Minda."

"I'm Mando. Would you dance with me?" The man gently showed his hand.

Minda directly stared and slowly touched the lines of his palm. The sparkle in her loving eyes hinted at her assumption that the romantic encounter was bound to happen.

"It's written in your palm, and I feel safe in your hand." Minda sweetly whispered.

Mando grinned from ear to ear, and strongly seized her delicate hand. They danced the night away in their first meeting. They began to show up each evening the gymnasium held a disco, and romanced each other for years.

Minda and Mando partnered for a slow dance, but she seemed bothered as he quietly pressed and scrubbed her arm. Mando gave Minda a disturbed look. He apparently tried to maintain the uncomfortable silence between them, but he eventually gave up.

"I have loved you for years, but you've never let me see you in daylight. What's wrong, Minda?" He asked in a begging voice.

She heavily shook her head and abruptly avoided his eyes.

He gently continued. "Your skin feels different. I've been asking you about it, but you've always refused to answer. It's fine with me if you use powder. You don't need to hide anything from me."

"So what do you want to happen?!" She blurted angrily.

He calmly replied. "Please see me tomorrow morning. I'll be here."

The party lights and the party music gradually died as they were replaced by the sunlight from the morning sky and the silence of the woodland.

Mando patiently stood at the center of the open gymnasium, as hope shone in his handsome face. He effortlessly recalled the countless nights he intimately spent with Minda, until he anticipatedly heard light footsteps.

"Mando." A woman's voice uttered.

He widely grinned and energetically turned around. In front of her, his mouth suddenly turned down and his eyes visibly turned dim. Mando saw the woman he loved for years, in daylight for the first time. Before him was Minda who had patches of thick red skin and silvery scales.

With hatred and frustration in her voice, she spoke. "I've always known you won't love me for what I am."

Minda weakly turned her back and slowly walked away, until she disappeared in the woodland, which was enlivened by the pending evening.

The bright and loud disco began, and to the surprise of the crowd, countless white winged creatures flew from the dark and danced under the warm spotlight.

The strange yet bewitching sight reminded them of Minda who disappeared forever.

Anita the Ant

Deep stinging pain instantly cut her heavily grieving bosom. She consciously realized that the present moment would be her last glimpse of her husband's dead face, beneath the clear glass of a shiny white coffin.

Her melancholic face, aged by half of a century, hardened as she apparently attempted to regain her composure. However, weighty tears swiftly formed in her exhausted eyes, and unstoppably cascaded down her pale cheeks.

She seemingly appeared as a mourning widow, in pristine white dress, who emotionally wished for her deceased husband to be miraculously brought back to earthly life. However, within her unspoken thoughts, she clearly began to bitterly recall the maltreatment and abuse she painfully experienced from him.

His cruel fists formed dark bruises in her powerless body. His harsh mouth formed aching memories in her shameful mind. The seemingly irreparable annihilation, which he violently caused on her frail character, evidently remained in her human existence during his cold burial.

Her transparent tears were secretly produced by profound relief and uplifting freedom, which she ultimately felt when her husband's hard coffin was utterly closed. However, a familiar romantic emotion transpired in her inmost feminine core, when her surprised eyes fully laid on the radiant face of a young man who seemingly stood with glory and purity before her.

"I'm sorry for your loss. I offer my condolences to you, Anita." He said in a comforting tone.

"Thank you. Thank you, Antonio." She mindlessly replied.

He was about to turn his back when she delightfully whispered. "We are now free, Antonio."

His loving eyes brightened as his head slowly nodded. "Yes, Anita. We are now free. Free to love each other. Free to begin our forever."

In a silent corner of the ordinary cemetery, two living hearts profoundly rejoiced together. Antonio and Anita embraced and kissed each other passionately. Their intertwined souls seemingly experienced the boundless bliss of their desired eternity.

All of a sudden, a thunderous masculine voice shattered their shared heaven. "Mister Antonio!"

Their secret affair was doubtlessly revealed as an infuriated police team extremely shocked them.

Their sinful crime vividly came back to their murderous minds, and their sheer guilt distinctly told them that the exact present was the fear-inducing and deathly moment for both of them to pay the price.

The chief sternly continued. "Mister Antonio, you're under arrest!"

The lightning blindly flashed, the thunder deafeningly clapped, and the rain massively poured. The police team harshly separated the star-crossed lovers despite their fierce resistance.

"Please, let him go! Let Antonio go! Arrest me instead. It was me! It was me who poisoned my husband." Anita hopelessly begged and shamelessly admitted.

"No! It was my plan. Arrest me! Leave Anita alone." Antonio intensely pleaded.

The police team forcefully dragged Antonio who mindlessly turned submissive. Anita severely sobbed and drastically weakened.

She thoughtlessly lay on the grassy ground, and resoundingly screamed in fatal pain. Her physical body was terribly pulverized by unseen yet mighty forces, and her tiny particles horribly formed into red insects that bore sharp stings that signified the stinging pain which she was substantially made up of.

Winona the Worm

The lingering kitchen smells enticed several customers to regularly dine in the restaurant hut. Gleaming tables were cheerfully cleaned by lively neat janitors. Mouth-watering dishes were promptly served by amiable uniformed waiters. The crowded place was normally filled with the mixed sounds of sizzling foods, clanking utensils, and chattering diners.

A slender tall waitress gave a sensuous stare to a good-looking man who was leisurely consuming his sumptuous dinner. The seemingly instinctive man suddenly noticed the sexual motive consciously displayed by the flirtatious waitress.

The shameless waitress was about to intentionally come near the surprised man when another woman vibrantly appeared next to her object of interest. The other woman instantly grabbed the man's undivided attention by playfully touching his masculine hand and loudly kissing his handsome face.

The other woman, who assuredly acted as the man's lover, boldly glared at the jealous waitress. The two mad feminine spirits drastically made the ordinary atmosphere intensely clashing. However, the defeated heart was immediately revealed, when the man abruptly stood up and lovingly put his strong arm around the other woman. The sweet lovers happily exited from the restaurant hut.

Extreme pain was shown in the teary eyes of the defeated waitress, but her reddish lips gradually curved into a sinister smile. Her trembling hand slowly moved inside her skirt pocket and firmly pulled out a filled bottle of love potion. The witchy waitress deliberately stared at the magical drink and assuredly whispered, "You'll be mine, Valentin. You'll love Winona alone."

Several days and nights naturally arrived, but no Valentin reappeared in the restaurant hut. Winona evidently grew impatient and desperate, as she constantly glared at the open door.

The full moon brightly shone in the evening cloudless sky when light footsteps became clearly audible in the unusually empty restaurant hut. Winona quickly lifted her head and anticipatedly laid her eyes on Valentin.

"A glass of red wine, please." Valentin nonchalantly requested.

Winona quickly prepared Valentin's order. Valentin wordlessly sat in a wooden chair, as Winona secretly poured her love potion in the glass of red wine. The waitress wickedly smiled and excitedly placed the filled glass on a wine tray. She gradually turned around and showed an innocent face to the unknowing customer.

Winona calmly served the red wine, mixed with her love potion, to her object of interest. She stood still in front of Valentin to consciously watch him slowly sipped the red wine. The wineglass was eventually emptied and Winona's focused eyes sparked in success.

Valentin suddenly had a strange sexual aura as he anticipatedly lifted his head to directly stare at Winona. The mindless Valentin swiftly stood up and aggressively possessed the submissive Winona. Their carnal affair secretly lasted for countless nights that constantly fulfilled the overjoyed waitress.

The full moon was gradually covered by thick clouds when Valentin suddenly stopped kissing Winona. A terrible shock bulged his guilty eyes. Winona speedily understood the perilous moment and instantly pulled out her filled bottle.

"Drink this!" Winona wildly forced Valentin to drink the love potion.

"No! Stop!" Valentin strongly resisted Winona.

All of a sudden, a trembling feminine hand mightily grabbed the magical drink from the fierce Winona. The shocked waitress abruptly felt confused when she unexpectedly saw Valentin's lover. The mad woman wildly threw the filled bottle that resoundingly shattered on the wooden floor. The love potion fully splattered and Winona horribly retaliated.

Winona speedily attacked Valentin's lover. "Valentin is mine! Valentin is mine alone!"

Upon intensely witnessing his defeated lover, Valentin eventually recovered from his terrible shock. He mightily rescued his frail lover from Winona's beastly hands.

"Stop hurting my lover!" Valentin angrily shouted at the surprised Winona.

Winona instantly looked deranged and forcefully cried. "I love you, Valentin!"

Valentin firmly and assuredly spoke. "I choose my lover over you, Winona."

The reunited lovers swiftly turned their back and exited from the restaurant hut. The abandoned Winona heavily sobbed. Her exhausted eyes blankly rested on a poison bottle and her shaking hand swiftly seized the deathly object.

Winona forcefully opened the poison bottle and boldly drank the contained liquid. Her entire body horribly trembled and suddenly collapsed. The brightness of the full moon, uncovered by thick clouds, completely enveloped the lifeless Winona. When the silver moonlight faded, slender long creatures wormed on the filthy floor of the restaurant hut.

Selene the Snail

Hectares of abundant rice plantations were joyously filled with vigorous male farmers. They were firmly holding sharp sickles as they were vibrantly reaping a rich harvest.

An aged man whose veiny hands resting on his hard walking cane silently watched the working men. The noticeable light of satisfaction was certainly shown in his fixed eyes.

The apparent farm owner weakly stood next to a young lady who was seemingly the immature and female resemblance of his seasoned visage. The obvious expression of naivety clearly appeared in her delicate face.

The aged farm owner whose eyes turned dim spoke with a hoarse voice. "Selene, I wish you could inherit the land. But you are not a man. You can't lead these men. You can't manage the plantations. Oh, I wish I was given a son. But how unfortunate I am."

The words of disappointment Selene evidently heard from her own father triggered indignation in her feminine core. However, she strongly remained tight-lipped with an air of composure.

Her pained father continued. "When you get married, your husband will inherit my land. Because he is the man. But you will lose our name. No one will know me anymore. Why aren't you speaking, Selene?"

With irritation in her voice, Selene spoke. "What should I say, Father? Is there anything I should say? You have prohibited me from speaking my mind. I don't even know if I have a mind. So how would I speak?"

Her father angrily raised his voice. "How rude you are, Selene! I shouldn't have asked you to speak. You lack delicacy and brains. You should get married soon. To a man who is a farm owner like me. So my land won't go to waste."

The aged man slowly walked away, feebly leaving his hurt daughter behind. Selene's teary eyes wandered from a working male farmer to another. She subtly looked like in desperate search of someone whom she secretly knew. All of a sudden, her face brightened in delight as she fixed her hopeful eyes on one of the men.

Selene wholeheartedly exclaimed. "Samuel!"

Samuel was utterly surprised when he lifted his head and saw Selene. The rest of the working farmers confusingly turned their heads and talked in whispers. Selene, who seemed blind to perceive the unfavorable situation, happily ran toward Samuel.

Samuel stammered in fear. "What are you doing, Miss Selene?"

With pride in her voice, Selene loudly spoke. "I just want everyone to know that I'm in love with you, Samuel. I love you! And I will marry you! I will marry you, Samuel!"

The rest of the working farmers turned dead silent, as Samuel gravely felt shame in his poor spirit. He steadily bowed his head as his young aura turned stone cold. Upon seeing his unfavorable change, Selene's soul was swallowed by extreme guilt.

With pity in her voice, she whispered. "I'm sorry, Samuel."

Without any little courage to lift his head, he secretly uttered. "I will die without you, Miss Selene. But I will also die if I'll be with you. So I'll end everything here."

Samuel suddenly raised his sharp sickle and swiftly moved it to his exposed neck. With sheer shock in Selene's eyes, Samuel beheaded himself.

The alarmed fearful male farmers wildly fled from the unexpected and horrible death scene.

Selene instantly heard the loud voice of his aged father. "What a scene you made, Selene!"

She stood still but eventually picked the blood-stained sickle. She gradually turned her trembling body to madly face her confused father.

With tears of despair cascading from her burning eyes, she spoke in sheer resentment. "You ruined my life! Now, I will ruin yours!"

Selene's aged father felt the pending devastation, as he fearfully begged. "Don't do what you're thinking, Selene."

Selene remained untamed. "I curse the land where my head shall fall."

She readily bowed her head, and like Samuel, she deliberately beheaded herself. As her head fell, her father's cane dropped.

After the terrible circumstance, shelled creatures gradually emerged and plagued hectares of rice plantations, which the farmers firmly believed as the drastic impact of Selene's curse.

Bathilda the Bat

In the secluded mountainous region of the young expansive world, a primitive tribe secretly inhabited the seemingly unwelcoming wilderness.

The aboriginal tribe was proudly headed by a female tribal chief that painfully birthed a female infant at the exact time the male tribal chief eventually died of old age.

The new mother thoughtfully gave her newborn baby the name of Bathilda. She quietly placed her delicate daughter in her arms that were scarred by beastly encounters.

She rigidly raised and cruelly trained the adolescent Bathilda to superiorly master hunting ancient animals with the merciless use of deathly spears.

Every unfortunate moment Bathilda unwittingly missed her innocent prey, her aging mother fiercely battered her with the lengthy solid spears.

The miserable Bathilda constantly sought comfort and peace in a remote mountain cave as she agonizingly tried to fully heal her physical wounds with raw leaves.

The expected tribal heiress gradually grew into a battle-scarred woman as she utterly embraced her primeval existence by habitually slaughtering suspected human invaders.

The dead of night was normally illuminated by bonfires that ordinarily produced cracking noises that the lonesome adult Bathilda regularly observed.

A rare moment unanticipatedly occurred to Bathilda when her gray mother, the tribal chief, quietly showed up amid her solitude.

With a raspy voice, her mother spoke. "Bathilda, you ought to pick a man to be your mate. You ought to bear a child and head our tribe with him. We shall hold a competition to see the man that you and the tribe deserve."

In a firm tone, Bathilda answered. "No man can match my strength and mind. No man can win my love and my father's tribe. I can head the tribe alone."

Her provoked mother asserted. "You need a child, Bathilda. You shall grow old like me hereafter. You shall need a mate as strong as your father was."

Bathilda matched her mother's anger. "Never use my father against me. You can't speak for him. I ought to think on my own. You only think for the tribe, never for me. I have been living in my own strength, so I need no man when you die of old age."

The female tribal chief retaliated. "How disrespectful you are, Bathilda!"

She swiftly picked a lengthy solid spear to intentionally strike her unruly daughter, but Bathilda was agile to avoid the expected attack.

Bathilda effortlessly smirked. "You are old now, Mother."

The expected tribal heiress gracefully lifted a burning torch, quickly turned her back, and anticipatedly sheltered herself in her dearest cave.

However, in utter surprise, Bathilda saw a foreign man inside her treasured territory. She was about to fiercely attack the suspected invader, with the flaming fire on her wooden torch, when the man suddenly raised his hands as an obvious sign of surrender.

The foreign man spoke in fright. "I am not an enemy. I am only seeking shelter. I shall leave when the sun rises."

Bathilda slowly regained her composure as she stared straight to the innocent eyes of the man.

She pleasantly asked. "Do you have a name?"

The man calmed down and gently nodded. "I am Benedict."

She sweetly smiled and introduced herself. "I am Bathilda. You are now safe with me. But I fear when my tribe sees you. They will certainly hurt you. So just stay here. With me. And no one can harm you."

Benedict instantly sensed the sexual attraction Bathilda ignorantly felt for him. He slowly walked toward her and suddenly kissed her. She unknowingly dropped the burning torch, and the entire cave ultimately succumbed to utter darkness.

For countless nights, Benedict secretly stayed in Bathilda's cave as the tribal woman diligently served him ancient animals for food.

Inside the remote mountain cave, Bathilda silently cut her forearm with a sharp stone and dropped her blood on a fresh leaf. Benedict slowly imitated Bathilda, and mixed his blood with hers. The tribal woman and the foreign man gradually sipped their united bloods.

All of a sudden, a wild fire blazed before Bathilda and Benedict. The female tribal chief fiercely showed up with the whole enraged tribe with her.

Bathilda's mother spoke in sheer madness. "Kill the invader!"

Bathilda instantly stood between Benedict and the tribe as she emotionally protested. "No! I order you not to harm him. Benedict has won my love. And with me, he shall head our tribe. Mother, I now have inside me your grandchild."

The female tribal chief was extremely stupefied but eventually shook her head in madness.

Bathilda's mother furiously reiterated. "Kill the invader!"

When the enraged tribe was about to attack in unison, a lengthy solid spear shockingly perforated Bathilda from the back to the chest. When the tribal woman was falling dead, Benedict's hands gradually released the deathly spear.

Benedict fearlessly spoke. "Now, kill me!"

The tribe went wild as they mercilessly attacked the foreign man, and they eventually dragged the lifeless Benedict outside Bathilda's cave.

The female tribal chief forcefully plucked the cold spear from her daughter's dead body, and silently laid the lifeless Bathilda inside the mountain cave of utter darkness.

The horrible memory remained in the minds of the primitive tribe, as dark-colored winged creatures showed up from Bathilda's cave and flew in the unwelcoming wilderness every night.

About the Author

Ancel Mondia

Ancel Mondia was awarded Fiction - Woman Writer of the Year by Ukiyoto Publishing for her title Nene's Prose. She also authored Tula ni Nene, Nene's Poetry and Ikalawang Koleksyon.

www.ingramcontent.com/pod-product-compliance
Lightning Source LLC
LaVergne TN
LVHW041602070526
838199LV00046B/2100